Enid Blyton ™

The Magic Treacle Jug

Illustrated by Pam Storey

Illustrations copyright © 1997 Grandreams Ltd
This edition published 2002
© Robert Frederick Ltd., 4 North Parade, Bath
Printed in China

Now once when Miggle the goblin was walking home at night through Goblin Village, he saw a light in Mother Tick-Tock's cottage window. He stopped and thought for a moment.

"I think I'll go and peep in," he said to himself. "Mother Tick-tock's grandfather was a wizard and it's said that she knows plenty of useful spells. I might see something interesting if I go and peep."

So he crept into the front garden and peeped in at the window. Mother Tick-Tock was there, cutting large slices of bread, one after the other.

"I suppose those are for her children's supper," thought Miggle, counting them. "One, two, three, four, five, six, seven – yes, they are. Goodness me – does she give them just dry bread for their suppers, poor things?"

He watched carefully. He saw Mother Tick-Tock take up a small blue jug and he heard her speak to it.

"Pour me treacle, strong and sweet,
For a Very Special Treat!"

And, to Miggle's surprise, the jug left Mother Tick-Tock's hand, poised itself above a slice of bread and poured out good, thick, yellow treacle! Then it balanced itself above the next slice and poured more treacle. Then it went to the third slice.

"Good gracious me! How can a little jug like that hold so much treacle!" thought Miggle, in surprise. "Look at it, pouring thickly over one slice after another. What lovely treacle too! Ooh, I wish I had some of it!"

Mother Tick-Tock suddenly caught sight of Miggle's face at the window and, leaving the jug pouring treacle on the last slice of all, she ran to the window, shouting angrily. Miggle disappeared at once and ran home at top speed. He was afraid of Mother Tick-Tock.

But he couldn't forget that wonderful Treacle-Jug. To think of having sweet treacle at any time!

How lucky Mother Tick-Tock's children were. No wonder he so often saw them about with thick slices of bread and treacle.

Now two days later Miggle made himself a fine pudding. But when he came to taste it he found that he had left out the sugar. Ooooh – how horrid it was!

"Now, if only I could borrow that Treacle-Jug!" thought Miggle, longingly. "I could have treacle all over my pudding and it would be one of the nicest I'd ever had. I wonder if Mother Tick-Tock would lend me the jug."

Just at that very moment Miggle saw someone passing his cottage and who should it be but Mother Tick-Tock herself, on her way to visit a friend,

Mrs. Know-A-Lot. Miggle watched her go down the road and a small thought uncurled itself in his mind.

"Couldn't I just borrow the Treacle-Jug for a few minutes? Nobody would ever know. And if it's a magic jug, the treacle would never,

never come to an end, so it wouldn't matter my having just a very little!"

He sat and thought about it, looking at his sugarless pudding. Then he popped it back into the oven to keep warm and ran out of the front door very quickly indeed. "I must get that jug before I change my mind!" he thought. "I'll use it to cover my pudding with treacle, then I'll take it straight back. Run, Miggle, run!"

He came to Mother Tick-Tock's cottage. The door was locked, but the window was open just a crack – a big enough crack for a small goblin to put in a bony little arm and reach to the shelf for a small blue jug! There!

He had got it. But how strange – it was quite empty!

"I'd better not go too fast with it, in case I fall and break it," he thought. So he put it under his coat and walked back slowly. He felt very excited indeed.

He stood the blue jug on his table and fetched his pudding from the oven. "Ha, pudding – you're going to taste very nice in a minute!" he said, and set it down in the middle of his table. He picked up the jug and spoke to it solemnly, just as Mother Tick-Tock had.

"Pour me treacle, strong and sweet,
For a Very Special Treat!"

said Miggle. The little jug left his hand at once and poised itself over the pudding. It tilted and – to Miggle's great delight – a stream of rich golden

9

treacle poured out and fell on his pudding. Miggle's mouth began to water. Oooh! That pudding was going to taste very, very nice!

"There! That's enough, thank you, little Treacle-Jug," said Miggle at last. "Don't pour any more, or the treacle will spill out of the dish."

But the jug took no notice at all. It went on pouring steadily and Miggle saw that the treacle was now dripping over the edges of the pudding-dish. "Hey! Didn't you hear what I said!" he cried. "Stop, jug!

You'll ruin my tablecloth!"

But the jug didn't stop. It still hung there in the air, treacle pouring from its little spout. Miggle was angry. He snatched at the jug, but it hopped away in the air and went on pouring in another place.

"Stop, jug! Don't pour treacle into my armchair!" shouted Miggle. "Oh my goodness! Look what you've done! Emptied treacle all over the seat of my chair and the cushion! Come away from there!"

He snatched at the jug again, but it wouldn't let itself be caught. It got away from his grabbing hand just in time and hung itself up in the air just above the wash-tub, which was full of Miggle's dirty clothes, soaking in the suds there.

"Hey!" cried Miggle in alarm. "Not over my washing, for goodness'

sake! Stop, I say! Don't you see what you're doing? You're not supposed to pour treacle over chairs and wash-tubs, only over puddings and tarts! Oh, you mischievous jug! Wait till I get you! I'll break you in half!"

He snatched at the jug again, but it swung away in the air and this time hung itself over the nice new hearth-rug.

Trickle, trickle, trickle – the rich, sticky treacle poured down steadily over the rug, and poor Miggle tried to pull it away. But he soon found himself standing in treacle, for it spread gradually over the floor.

Then Miggle began to feel very alarmed indeed. What was he to do with this mad Treacle-Jug? He simply MUST stop it somehow!

"Ah – I've an idea!" thought Miggle. "Where's my fishing net? I'll get that and catch the jug in it. Then I'll smash it to bits on the ground. Oh, this treacle! How I hate walking in it! It's just like glue!"

He made his way to the corner where he kept his net and took hold of it. At once the Treacle-Jug swung itself over to him and poured treacle down on his head and face. How horrible! How sticky! Miggle was so angry that he shouted at the top of his voice.

13

"I'll smash you! I'll break you into a hundred pieces!" He swung the fishing net at the jug and almost caught it. It seemed frightened and swung away out of the door and up the stairs, pouring treacle all the way. Miggle sat down and cried most bitterly. Whatever was he to do?

Soon he heard a curious glug-glug noise and he looked up in alarm. A river of treacle was flowing slowly down the stairs! It flowed through the kitchen and out of the door, down the path and into the street. People passing by were quite astonished.

Mother Tick-Tock, coming back from visiting her friend, was astonished too. But she knew in a trice what had happened.

"Miggle's borrowed my Treacle-Jug!" she said. "I saw him peeping through the window when I used it the other night. The mean, thieving little fellow!"

Miggle saw Mother Tick-Tock and waded out through the treacly river to his front gate, crying, "Please, Mother Tick-Tock, I'm sorry. I can't make this jug stop pouring. Is there a spell to stop it as well as to start it?"

"Of course there is," said Mother Tick-Tock. "It's just as well to know both spells if you steal something like a Treacle-Jug, Miggle. Well, you can keep the jug if you like. I've a much bigger one I can use. How tired of treacle you must be, Miggle!"

"Oh, Mother Tick-Tock, please, please take your jug away," begged Miggle, kneeling down in the treacle. "I'll do anything, if you only will!"

"Very well. If you come and dig my garden for me all the year round and keep it nice, I'll stop the jug from pouring and take it back," said Mother Tick-Tock. Miggle groaned. He did so hate gardening!

"I'll come," he said. "I don't want to, but I will."

"If you don't, I'll send the jug to pour over your head," said Mother Tick-Tock and everyone laughed. She called loudly, "Treacle-Jug, come here!"

The little blue jug sailed out of a bedroom window and hung over Miggle's head. He dodged away at once. Mother Tick-Tock chanted loudly,

"Be empty, jug, and take yourself
Back to your place upon my shelf!"

And – hey presto – the Treacle-Jug became quite empty, turned itself upside-down to show Mother Tick-Tock that it had obeyed her and then flew swiftly through the air on the way to her cottage. Mother Tick-Tock

knew she would find it standing quietly in its place on her kitchen-shelf.

"Well, good-bye, Miggle," she said. "You've quite a lot of cleaning up to do, haven't you? Somehow I don't think you'll want to eat treacle again in a hurry!"

She was right. Poor old Miggle can't even see a treacle-tin now without running for miles! And I'm not a bit surprised at that!